The Reading Agency inspires people of all ages and backgrounds to read for pleasure and empowerment. They run the Summer Reading Challenge in partnership with libraries, as well as supporting reading groups in schools and libraries all year round. Find out more and join your local library. **summerreadingchallenge.org.uk**

World Book Day also facilitates fundraising for:

Book Aid International, an international book donation and library development charity. Every year, they provide one million books to libraries and schools in communities where children would otherwise have little or no opportunity to read. **bookaid.org.uk**

Read for Good, who motivate children in schools to read for fun through its sponsored read, which thousands of schools run on World Book Day and throughout the year. The money raised provides new books and resident storytellers in all of the UK's children's hospitals. **readforgood.org**

*Đ1.50 in Ireland

MR. MEN™ LITTLE MISS™ © THOIP (a SANRIO company)

My Book About Me by Mr. Silly © 2018 THOIP (a SANRIO company)
Printed and published under licence from Price Stern Sloan, Inc., Los Angeles.
Published in Great Britain by Egmont UK Limited
The Yellow Building, 1 Nicholas Road, London W11 4AN
ISBN 978 1 4052 9086 9
68608/1
Printed in Italy

Stay safe online. Egmont is not responsible for content hosted by third parties.

MY BOOK ABOUT ME
by Mr. Silly

Original concept by
Roger Hargreaves

Written and illustrated by
Adam Hargreaves

EGMONT

Mr Silly wanted to make a book.

"Now, what can I write about?" he said to himself.

He took a sip from his mug of hot toast.

"I know! I can write about me!" he suddenly declared.

So Mr Silly got a pad of paper and began.

He dipped a carrot in a pot of ink and began to write.

Messily.

It is not easy to write with a carrot, but Mr Silly did not use a pen.

That would be far too sensible!

He wrote down the title:

'My Book About Me.'

And then he wrote about the time he went to the Nonsenseland Bookshop.

And bought a book.

One page …

… at a time!

It took a very long time to buy it.

But then Mr Silly changed his mind.

Just writing about himself might be a bit boring.

I would disagree, but Mr Silly had made his mind up.

Or was that down?

You never can tell with Mr Silly.

He decided he would include his friends in his book.

If his friends were in his book then they would want to read it.

First of all he wrote about Mr Wrong.

Mr Wrong reads his books upside down.

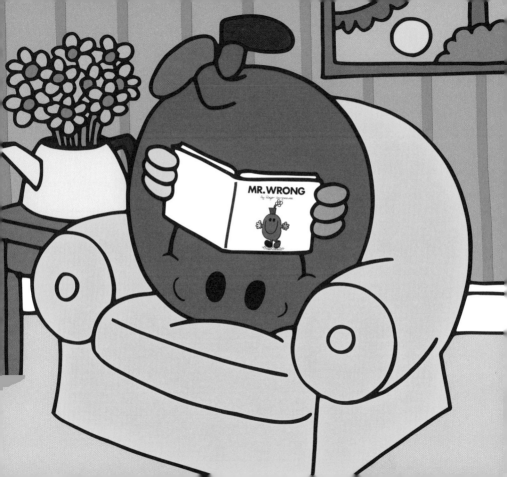

Whereas Mr Topsy-Turvy reads his books back to front.

So he would begin with the ending and end with the beginning!

How topsy-turvy!

Mr Silly wrote about Mr Greedy and his many cookery books.

And Little Miss Magic and her amazing book of spells.

Then there was a chapter on Mr Busy.

A very short chapter.

Mr Busy is too busy to ever finish a book.

Finally, Mr Silly wrote about Mr Happy.

Well, it is always nice to finish with a happy ending!

Mr Silly was very pleased with his story.

He decided to invite round all his friends who were going to be in his book for the big reveal.

But first he had to make it.

He went out to his shed and took down a saw and a hammer and a box of nails.

Which was odd.

It took him all night long to make the book.

Mr Silly's book was big.

As big as a house.

With a door.

Mr Silly opened the door and invited everyone in.

"Welcome to my book," he said.

"I have something to announce," he continued.

"You will be very pleased to hear that you will all be famous because ..."

My name is Mr. Silly and this is a book all about me and my friends.

li... a very silly ho...

n... ...try call...

...land...

"… you are now all IN my book!"

How very silly.

WORLD **BOOK** DAY

We hope you enjoyed this book.

Proudly brought to you by **WORLD BOOK DAY**,

the **BIGGEST CELEBRATION** of the **magic** and **fun** of **storytelling**.

We are the **bringer of books to readers** everywhere

and a **charity** on a **MISSION** to take you on a **READING JOURNEY**.

EXPLORE new worlds (and bookshops!)

EXPAND your imagination

DISCOVER some of the very best authors and illustrators with us.

A **LOVE OF READING** is one of life's greatest gifts.

And this book is **OUR gift to YOU.**

HAPPY READING. HAPPY WORLD BOOK DAY!

WORLD BOOK DAY

SHARE A STORY

Discover and share stories from breakfast to bedtime.

HERE'S HOW:

1 VISIT YOUR LOCAL BOOKSHOP

Your go-to destination for awesome reading recommendations and events with your favourite authors and illustrators.

 booksellers.org.uk/ bookshopsearch

2 JOIN YOUR LOCAL LIBRARY

Browse and borrow from a huge selection of books, get expert ideas of what to read next and take part in wonderful family reading activities – all for FREE!

 findmylibrary.co.uk

3 GO ONLINE AT WORLDBOOKDAY.COM

Fun podcasts, activities, games, videos, downloads, competitions, new books galore and all the latest book news.